Jacob's Cats

Paws & Poetry
20 Whisker-Worthy Rhymes

by Janice Pedder

Published in 2024
by Janice Pedder

ISBN: 978-1-913898-90-8

Cover and Book interior Design
by Russell Holden
www.pixeltweakspublications.com

"Jacob's Cats" was started during the pandemic lockdown. Jacob is my youngest grandchild, and he lived with his Mum who worked at home. School lessons were sent through computers or mobile phones. Jacob couldn't visit his other relations, aunts and cousins, and he couldn't pop round to his other grandparents or his Dad, and I lived a distance away. His friends were stuck in their own homes for a while, and there were no games of football played on the school field.

So Jacob had to amuse himself most of the time. I also had to find different things to do. I decided to take some photos of local cats, and then I wondered if I could write rhymes to tell their stories. I realised that I could post the first poem and picture so that Jacob could receive the unexpected surprise. Looking back I started with "Anton's Crunchy Biscuits", followed by "Poison" and then "Belle."

As time crawled onwards, I contacted my friends by email and asked if pictures of their cats could be sent to me. People I knew were pleased to assist me, and cat owners that I didn't know sent many photos, so more rhymes and illustrations went onto the pages of "Jacob's Cats".

Eventually the lockdown lifted and Jacob (by now he was nearly 12) visited his friend's houses and took pictures with his mobile phone, then he emailed the pictures to me.

Gradually the book took shape and eventually there were 20 poems, all splendidly different because the cats were all different. Even if they looked the same their personalities were unique.

Everyone that looks through the book always chooses the cat they like the most. I too have a favourite, but I don't tell, just in case the other cats get "stroppy".

Many people assisted me with this book, but especially –

Joan C - a good friend and the best proofreader ever.

Nicola D - my next-door neighbour and friend who sorted out the lay-out on each page.

Debbie - from Leeds. How many times did I ask for different pictures?

Ron L - My partner and dependable rock. Little did he know that he would be swamped with unexpected cats!

Contents

Anton's Crunchy Biscuits 1
Belle 2
Black John 4
Daisy and Maisie 6
Kitty's Valentine To Her Owner 8
Jeremy Whizz 10
Hector 12
Jay 14
Poison 15
Princess 16
Larry 17
Minstrel 18
Thor 20
Grace 22
Oscar – Left in Charge 23
Good Queen Bess 24
Trainer 26
Nosey Rosie. 27
Pearl and Dolly 28
Waiting For A Name 30

A Word From Kitty

These rhymes were composed by the lady of the house and it was a surprise for me when I realised that she could push words into lines that rhymed. And they made sense. Of course she still had to make sure that my meals would arrive in the kitchen and my bowls were always washed.

Upstairs there is a large box on a table and the-man-who-thinks-he's-in-charge sorts out lots of numbers that I don't understand.

However, I am the inspiration for "Jacob's Cats" and without my input the book would never have been finished. It might be of interest to readers that the lady of the house hinted that "Ella's Cats" is now being put together, and the layout is slightly different. But she's keeping everything else a secret!

And now I will conclude, (posh word for finishing).

ONWARDS FELINES ONWARDS!

Anton's Crunchy Biscuits

Crunchy Biscuits in my dish,
Sometimes Chicken, sometimes Fish.
Crunchy Biscuits for my tea,
Lots of biscuits all for me.

At breakfast and at supper time,
Crunchy Biscuits, they're all mine.
Crunchy Biscuits, "Yum, yum, yum",
Crunchy Biscuits in my tum!

Belle

If ever you feel poorly
You need a cat like Belle.
A quiet cat, a calming cat,
She knows when you're not well.
She's just a little bunch of love,
A friend that sits and purrs.
And just to make sure you're alright
She puts her head near yours.

If you're feeling really down
And everything looks blue.
Belle will knead you with her paws,
And mew "I'm here for you."
When your friends are not around,
And you are on your own,
Belle will come and play with you,
And purr, "You're not alone".

If you have a horrid dream
And wake up in a fright.
Belle will be there straight away,
She's come to put things right.
Belle is just a fluffy cat,
A love-bucket of fur.
But she knows she belongs to you,
And you belong to her.

Black John

Black John is the Outlaw King who wanders through the night,
He patrols the quiet alleyways, he stays away from light.
He waits and listens to the sounds, whispering restless leaves
That dance across the tarmac, after dropping from the trees.

The night cats watch silently as Black John smells the air,
Mice are hiding in the walls but he really doesn't care.
He is waiting for a larger kill, a fight with vicious rats,
He knows he'll always triumph and, "That" he says, "Is that!"

Other cats are wary and often don't come near,
But Black John recognises them, there's nothing they should fear.
He's walked the streets for many years, he's taught them all to roam,
But as dawn breaks the order comes, "It's time we all go home."

At home he has nice blankets and a basket in the hall,
He oversees everything, he looks down at them all.
He prefers to sit up high, so he doesn't miss a thing,
He's powerful and he's clever, he's the Outlaw King.

WANTED!

BLACK JOHN

Daisy and Maisie

Two old lady cats, dozing in the sun
Dreaming of the long gone times when they were very young.
They climbed, they fought, adventures called, and life was noisy fun!

Daisy was the quiet cat, she always thought things through.
Where she'd go, the route she'd take, and what she'd find to do.
But Maisie had no plans at all, everything was new.

Maisie would stay out all day, but returned for her tea.
Daisy sat still by the door and waited so she'd see
Maisie run across the lawn, meowing, "Yes it's me!"

Now the days are soft and long and memories are gold.
Outdoors when it's warm and safe, indoors when it's cold.
Both cats think they're lucky, and they're happy being old.

Kitty's Valentine To Her Owner

I am here, you are there,
I sing to you from the bottom stair.
Yes! It's around ten past five –
It's breakfast time so look alive.

The food is good, you're doing fine;
I'll need some more at half past nine.
And then there's lunch, a pleasant snack,
I'll eat, go out and hurry back.

All afternoon I snooze and wait
For supper that I have at eight.
Then, while you watch the flashing box
I have a wash and clean my socks.

The evening passes, we are a pair.
We live together, I like to share
My life with you. I am your treasure,
It pleases me to give you pleasure.

Written by Kitty (Age 8.)

Jeremy Whizz

Jeremy Whizz is a skinny, brown cat.
He runs all the time and he never gets fat.
He runs out the door, he runs up the tree,
He runs round the garden, then rushes to me.

Jeremy Whizz sprints to his plate,
He gobbles his food, he simply can't wait.
He runs up the stairs and then he runs down,
And if he knew the way, he'd run to the town.

Jeremy Whizz goes out in the snow.
Sun, wind or rain, out he will go.
Jeremy's able to run and to roam,
Because he is clever, and always comes home.

Hector

When Hector was a kitten, he lived with Freddie Flynn.
He liked to fight with slippers, and he would always win.
He played out in the garden, he ran around the house,
He left Freddie lovely presents, a dead bird or a mouse.

When Hector was an adult cat Freddie went away.
Hector lived out on the street and he became a stray.
He searched for food and shelter, he was all alone,
But then a lady fed him and Hector found a home.

Now Hector is an old cat, and lives with Mary Grey.
He potters round her garden but likes to spend his day
Curled up on his cushion, his blanket, or her knee,
So Hector is looked after now and happy as can be.

Jay

Hot day, humid day, with very little breeze,
Our family sat outside underneath the trees.
And the only sound we heard was the buzz of wasps and bees.
Until
Our dogs started barking and they both ran inside
Followed by us. "What's up," we cried,
"It's under the cupboard, trying to hide."
And then
Dad put the dogs out: Mum found a light,
And we knelt on the floor and saw grey and white
A small, fluffy kitten, a-trembling with fright.
So
We gave it some water, and it drank the lot.
Then Mum picked it up and said, "What we've got
Is a kitten that's lost. And NO we are NOT
Keeping it.
We let people know about this small stray,
He wasn't claimed so he decided to stay.
And short of a name, we just called him Jay.
Quietly
Jay ruled our house with a soft, steady paw.
He got what he wanted and then yelled for more;
And even the dogs bent to Jay's law.
Memories
Are made as time spins away.
The two dogs went first, and that left just Jay
Who brought home a kitten, fluffy and grey.
His thanks
To our family at the end of his day.

Poison

Poison was a great big cat, as dark and black as night.
When he crept round a corner, someone got a fright.
His ears twitched, his tail raised, his gold eyes looked around,
And first he stood, and then he moved;- gone without a sound.

Poison lived deep in the woods. He spent his time alone.
He slept inside a hollow log, and this he called his home.
No squirrels, rabbits, mice or birds ever came nearby,
For Poison's claws were lethal; come near and you die.

Poison was quite famous, and people in the town
Boasted how they'd hunt him, and how they'd bring him down.
But no-one really tried to, although they talked for hours,
They realised he was special and had black magic powers.

Poison sometimes watched them rushing here and there.
Occasionally he'd be spotted, but Poison didn't care.
He glared at them, he stood up tall, he made them feel his might,
And then he hissed and disappeared, with nothing left but night.

Princess

Princess is an elegant cat
And sometimes she's a pest.
She knows she's smart and sassy,
Much better than the rest.
She rules the whole neighbourhood,
It's obvious she's the best.

Princess watches what occurs
She sees who comes and goes.
She keeps herself looking good
And likes to strike a pose.
Her fur is soft and beautiful
From her whiskers to her toes.

Princess sees the other cats
Hurtling here and there.
They screech and scream and yell all day,
They just don't seem to care.
But if they come too close to her
She tells them, "Don't you dare!"

Princess is the cat between,
She lives at number four.
Number three has two cats
And number five has more.
But Princess has given warning,
"Don't come in my door!"

Princess sits on the window sill
Watching the feline crowd.
She thinks they're rough and
scruffy,
They're common and so loud.
But she sits tall on the garden wall,
Elegant, regal and proud.

Larry

An old building site, rubble and stone,
That was the area that Larry called home.
Other cats lived there but not one had a name,
They fought and they hunted, every day was the same.

Larry was a traveller, he went from place to place.
He showed the scars from battles, and sores were on his face.
His foot was swollen, oozing blood, he limped across the ground.
He sank down on a pile of grit, but never made a sound.

"He's over here!" he heard a shout so he staggered to his feet.
"You'll be alright, we'll sort you out. Here's something good to eat."
They put him in a cardboard box with biscuits in a bowl.
He looked about, the biscuits called, and so he ate them all.

He learnt about needles, tablets, and creams. He was kept in a shed, warm and dry.
There were fluffy, soft blankets and clean water too, and salve for his very sore eye.
He liked being stroked and spoken to, by a lady who took him outside,
He explored the garden, there was a loud bang! He ran to his shed just to hide.

The shed was his safe place, quiet and still,
The garden his playground, he wandered at will.
Larry always remembered his hard life before
The fights and the wounds and how hunger would roar.
He ended his days looked after and fed,
With a soft, fluffy blanket, and his own cosy bed.

Minstrel

When I was chosen to be someone's pet
My mother made sure I would never forget
That Siamese cats are shrouded in mystery,
And my special line remembers our history.

We were the chosen cats, oriental and proud,
Intelligent, inquisitive, with a voice that was loud.
We guarded the temples, we were seen by the King,
We moved to the Palace, and we learnt how to sing.

We were beautifully coloured, soft cream and brown.
We watched when the tall ships arrived in the town.
We were traded for goods, then we sailed with the tide,
And we gradually travelled afar and world-wide.

We did have some hard times, we were foreign and strange,
People thought we were clever, but also deranged.
Some called us "Hell's felines" that wandered at night
And wailed in the darkness to give folks a fright!

And then there were breeders with fashions to follow,
Cuddly and fat, or skinny tomorrow.
Seal point, Chocolate point, Lilac and Blue,
We quietly progressed, and my line stayed true.

Thor

"We've always had a cat," said Gran,
"And the first of them was Thor.
When my Dad came home, a cat came too,
And they'd both survived the war.
Dad said they'd sailed the Arctic seas
Through biting winds and snow.
The crew worked shifts out on the deck
Then scurried down below.
From Liverpool to Russia,
Stopping at Scapa Flow.
Our ship was one of many
All waiting just to go.
Amid the heaven's turmoil,
The smoke, the shock, the fear,
Dad looked down and rubbed his eyes,
"What are you doing here?"
A black cat stood beside him,

It followed Dad around.
It stayed on deck, it went below,
It never made a sound.
Dad fed him, and he called him Thor,
Most times they were together
His yellow eyes mimicked the sun.
Thor ignored the awful weather.
Our destination was Murmansk,

A port where burly men
Unloaded all the cargo.
Then our ship set off again,
We sailed West towards our homes,
But not all made it back,
A German plane dropped its last bombs
A sudden, cruel attack.
We limped into Grimsby harbour,

There were stretchers in a long line.
There were mugs of tea and biscuits,
The sailors were told, “You’ll be fine.”
There were ambulances, doctors and nurses,
Who worked through the night and next day.
And in a side street a horse and cart waited
To take all the coffins away.
They found my Dad with shattered bones,

He was lying on the deck.
Towels were covering his lower limbs
And, like a scarf around his neck
Was his cat. “He goes with me,” ordered Dad,
“He’ll never need to roam .
His name is Thor, a Northern cat,
And together we’ll go home”.

Grace

I have an owner who likes me to purr
When I sit on her knee, she brushes my fur.
She looks after me and I'm company for her.

My owner decides what goes into my dish
Beef, turkey or chicken, but sometimes I wish
That my owner would like the smell of good fish.

Sometimes we play and I chase a soft ball,
Not a huge heavy thing, it's fluffy and small.
It's stored in a box at the back of the hall.

When I was much younger life was a race.
But now time moves slowly, a middle-aged pace.
And our names match our ages, she's Mary, I'm Grace.

Oscar – Left in Charge

"I was walking past the Christmas tree," said Oscar to his world,
"When the tinsel on the lowest branch suddenly unfurled,
And it wrapped itself around my tail, all sparkling and curled.

The red beads looked untidy so I tried to put them straight,
But they all stuck together and I worried about their weight.
And then they all fell on the floor, in a muddled state.

I know baubles are delicate, but they too crashed on the floor.
And three or four did shatter, but not too many more.
I piled them in a corner, away from the front door.

I was sitting being patient when a breeze came gusting through,
It blew the cards off the shelf and I wondered what to do.
I moved them to the corner and I waited here for you.

The Christmas lights are lovely, brightening up the night,
And Christmas decorations are such a wonderous sight.
Now you're home, all is well. And we can put things right."

Good Queen Bess

I am the ruler of abandoned slums
Small, scruffy streets that everyone shuns.
There is poverty here
With plenty to fear
And the fog of despair often comes.

I am the leader who walks through the night.
I take the young with me, their life will be bright.
I look for neat doors
That lead to clean floors
And windows that shine friendly light.

I am the Empress that persuaded the old
To leave the damp buildings held together by mould.
I found a large store,
Then two or three more
Where cats can forget endless cold.

I live near the slum streets, but I have a fine home,
A small cosy palace, a box for a throne.
I come home to rest
Humans know me as Bess.
But the cats call me Queen when I roam.

Trainer

Teaching humans in feline ways so a home runs as it should,
A cat in charge means proper homes are always feeling good.
It doesn't matter if floors are bare, but rooms need warmth and light,
Cats know best, they quietly nod, and know they'll make it right.

My humans learn quite slowly, they waste much of my time.
They think I belong to them, but really they are mine.
I started young and I soon learnt that my ways would be best,
To run a home is tiring, so I need lots of rest.

Cats make a home more comfortable, they have necessary rules.
Humans learn to do what's right, or they look like hopeless fools.
Dogs and other pets are nice so humans aren't alone,
But a cat develops clever paws, and they always rule the home.

Nosey Rosie.

Nosey Rosie spends her time watching the front door,
She likes to see the envelopes fall down to the floor,
Often there's one but sometimes there's three, maybe more.

When it's quiet upstairs she looks through the front window,
She can see all the cars and the vans down below.
And she wonders where all those people will go.

She looks round the kitchen, but she's emptied her dish,
She ate a large breakfast, just as she would wish
Then she waits for her supper, is it chicken or fish?

She likes the large couch though it shows wear and tear.
She dozes and dreams, then grooms her soft hair.
And she wonders if people will soon join her there.

Sometimes she listens and hears a faint knock,
Or there's a loud banging which gives her a shock!
But the best sound of all is the key in the lock...

Pearl and Dolly

Pearl was a very pretty cat, nice and slender, never fat,
Her fur was lovely silver-white, Pearl made sure she kept it bright.
She would nap but be aware if any other cat were there,
Her back would arch, her tail unfurl, "I'm in charge here," meowed Pearl.

Dolly was the other cat, she was greedy and quite fat.
She never tried to look her best, she washed a bit, then had a rest.
Her fur was shabby, brown and black, with a balding patch upon her back.
Her tummy bulged, she didn't care. She showed the signs of wear and tear.

Pearl liked to be left alone, she looked her best in a tidy home.
Dolly flopped down anywhere, anytime, she didn't care.
Pearl ignored her as best she could. She even growled, it did no good.
Dolly slept on and loudly snored. It didn't hurt to be ignored.

Then, out one day Pearl caught a chill, she shivered and felt really ill.
She curled up tightly on a chair, she coughed and then she was aware
Of a fluffy, round cat, fat and baggy, with a stomach that was very saggy,
Standing on the chair with her, gently licking Pearl's silver fur.

Dolly stayed with Pearl all night purring comfort to make things right.
And now the two cats are a pair, and Pearl has found she doesn't care
How scruffy Dolly looks some days, and yes she has some lazy ways,
But what will count from the new start is Dolly has a loving heart.

Waiting For A Name

He started life as William
But they shortened it to Bill.
Then they fancied Phillip
And of course they called him Phil.
But they passed him to a neighbour
Who decided he was Joe,
But he didn't respond to that name, so Joe would have to go.

No-one really wanted him
So he ran away.
He roamed the streets, the woods, the park
For somewhere else to stay.
One day he saw an open door, he quietly went inside.
He wandered round until he found a chair where he could hide.

Morning came, and to his surprise
He was offered food and care.
A lady lived all by herself,
And liked to have him there.
She fed him and she groomed him,
He sat upon her knee,
He purred and snuggled close to her and wondered what would be.

She told him they would choose a name
Especially for him.

She tried Bob, Dan and Cuthbert,
But ended up with Jim.
He liked to hear her say his name,
It meant he'd never roam.
He came running when she called, and Jim had found a home.

Name the cat!

How many of their names can you remember?

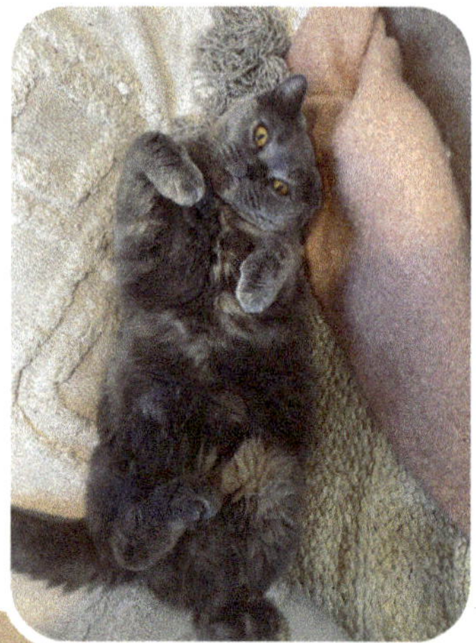

Milton Keynes UK
Ingram Content Group UK Ltd.
UKHW051113261024
450190UK00012B/123

9 781913 898908